Note to parents, carers and teachers

Read it yourself is a series of modern stories, favourite characters and traditional tales written in a simple way for children who are learning to read. The books can be read independently or as part of a guided reading session.

Each book is carefully structured to include many high-frequency words vital for first reading. The sentences on each page are supported closely by pictures to help with understanding, and to offer lively details to talk about.

The books are graded into four levels that progressively introduce wider vocabulary and longer stories as a reader's ability and confidence grows.

Ideas for use

- Although your child will now be progressing towards silent, independent reading, let her know that your help and encouragement is always available.

- Developing readers can be concentrating so hard on the words that they sometimes don't fully grasp the meaning of what they're reading. Answering the puzzle questions on pages 46 and 47 will help with understanding.

For more information and advice on Read it yourself and book banding, visit **www.ladybird.com/readityourself**

Book Band 10

Level 4 is ideal for children who are ready to read longer stories with a wider vocabulary and are eager to start reading independently.

Special features:

Full, exciting story

Clear type

Richer, more varied vocabulary

One day, my little sister Lola says, "Charlie, what is that book?"

I say, "It is a book about inventions. Me and Marv have to invent something for school."

10

11

Lola asks, "What is an invention?"

I say, "An invention is something new that helps people do things better and faster."

Marv says, "Like the telephone."

"But we already have a telephone," says Lola.

Longer sentences

12

13

Detailed illustrations to capture the imagination

Educational Consultant: Geraldine Taylor

Book Banding Consultant: Kate Ruttle

Text adapted by Jillian Powell
Text based on the script written by Carol Noble
Illustrations from the TV animation produced by Tiger Aspect Productions Limited

A catalogue record for this book is available from the British Library

First published by Ladybird Books Ltd MMXIII
80 Strand, London, WC2R ORL
A Penguin Company

This edition MMXV.

005

ISBN: 978-0-72329-373-6

Printed in China

I Am Inventing an Invention

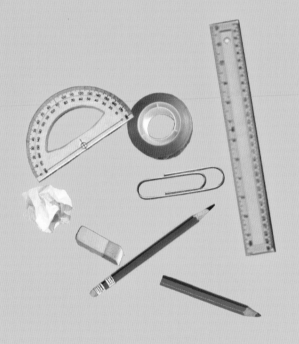

Characters created by
Lauren Child

My name is Charlie.

Me and my best friend Marv
like playing with Marv's
dog, Sizzles.

I have this little sister, Lola.
She is small and very funny.

She likes playing with her
best friend, Lotta.

One day, my little sister Lola says, "Charlie, what is that book?"

I say, "It is a book about inventions. Me and Marv have to invent something for school."

Lola asks, "What is an invention?"

I say, "An invention is something new that helps people do things better and faster."

Marv says, "Like the telephone."

"But we already have a telephone," says Lola.

I say, "Yes. But a very long time ago, there were no telephones."

Lola says, "No telephones? How would I tell Lotta about my new drawing?"

I say, "You would have to go and see Lotta."

"But that is a VERY long way," says Lola.

15

"I would have to go in the car with Mum," says Lola.

But I say, "Lola, a very long time ago, there were no cars. You would have to go by horse."

"Oh!" says Lola. "By horse?"

Lola says, "Cars and telephones are very good inventions. I am going to make an invention, too."

I say, "Lola, it is not easy to make a brilliant invention."

But Lola says, "I CAN! I can invent something. You'll see!"

"Marv," I say, "We must make a brilliant and useful invention not seen before."

And Marv says, "I've got it! How about something that can walk Sizzles for me?"

Lola looks at our drawing of
a dog bicycle. "But Sizzles
will not reach the pedals.
He is too small."

I say, "Oh, yes!"

"Well," says Marv. "It would
have been good."

I say, "We have to come up with
a new invention."

Then Lola says, "Look, Charlie. I am an inventor! I invented a crayon that is green AND blue."

"But what about red?" asks Marv.

Lola says, "Well... I have many more inventions. You'll see!"

"We must make a good invention, and fast," I say.

"It's not easy," says Marv. "All the good inventions have already been invented!"

Then I say, "I've got it!"

"We can make a brilliant apple picker-upper. It will pick up all the apples that come down from the trees."

So Marv asks, "What would it look like?"

I say, "It is made from two bicycles and a vacuum cleaner. If we pedal very fast, all the apples go into it then come out into the wheelbarrow."

I ask Mum if we can borrow the vacuum cleaner, but she says no.

"Oh no!" says Marv. "That was our best invention. Now what?"

Lola asks, "Have you come up with some good inventions?"

"Not one!" I say.

"Oh no," says Lola. "Maybe you are not inventors."

"But we have to invent something, fast," I say.

So we start inventing and Lola starts tidying up...

But before long, she gets stuck to everything with tape.

"Help! Get off! Oh no!"

Then Lola sees that everything
is stuck to her with tape.

"Look at me, Charlie. Everything
is stuck to me!"

I say, "Yes. Thank you for tidying
up, Lola."

But Lola says, "No, Charlie.
I am an inventor. See?
The pencils, crayons and clips
are all sticking to my dress.
There is a place for the pencils
and a place for the crayons and
for the clips. Everything is tidy."

41

Marv says, "Lola, that is brilliant!"

I say, "Can we borrow it for school?"

"But will people think it is REALLY useful?" asks Lola.

Marv says, "Yes!"

"And we think it is, too," I say.

Lola says, "I really am an inventor!"

Marv says, "What should we call your invention?"

Lola says, "The very brilliant and useful dress tidy-upper!"

How much do you remember about the story of I Am Inventing an Invention? Answer these questions and find out!

- Why do Charlie and Marv need to invent an invention?

- What do they invent first?

- Why won't that invention work?

- Which colours are in the crayon Lola invents?

- What doesn't Mum let Charlie borrow for his next invention?

- What does Lola call her brilliant last invention?

Unjumble these words to make the names of characters from the story, then match them to the correct pictures.

Carehli   Laol   Mrva

Ltoat   Szezisl

Read it yourself with Ladybird

Tick the books you've read!

For more confident readers who can read simple stories with help.

Level 3

 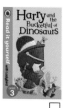  

Longer stories for more independent, fluent readers.

Level 4

The Read it yourself with Ladybird app is now available for iPad, iPhone and iPod touch

App also available on Android devices